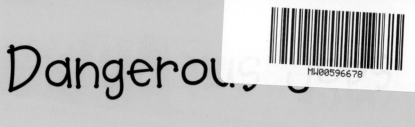

Dangerous

Written by Brylee Gibson

Rigby

DANGEROUS JOBS

Some people have jobs
that can be dangerous.
These are not jobs for everyone.
People who do dangerous jobs
have to be very careful,
because they could get hurt.

Fighting an oil fire.

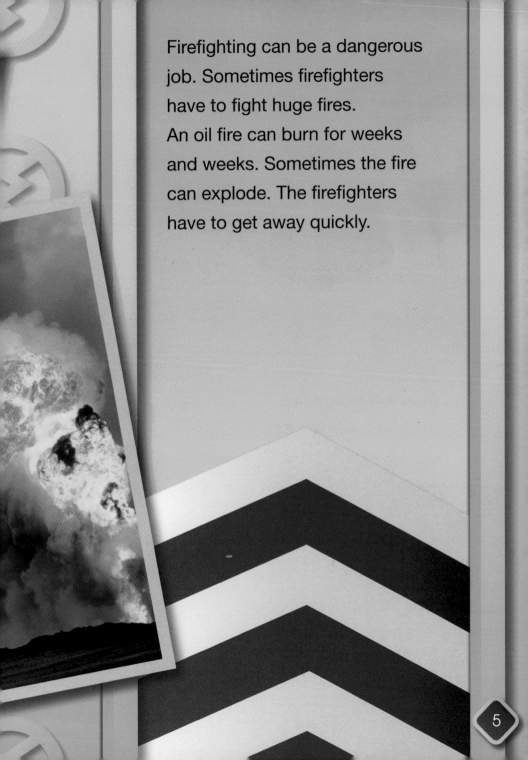

Firefighting can be a dangerous job. Sometimes firefighters have to fight huge fires. An oil fire can burn for weeks and weeks. Sometimes the fire can explode. The firefighters have to get away quickly.

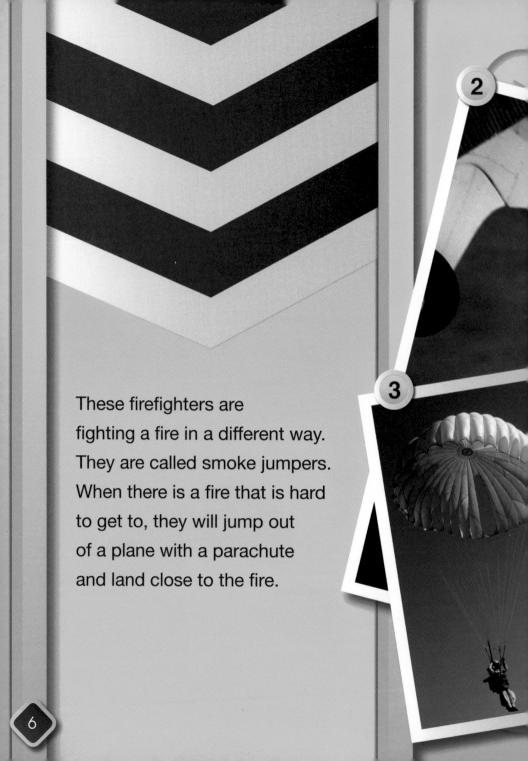

These firefighters are
fighting a fire in a different way.
They are called smoke jumpers.
When there is a fire that is hard
to get to, they will jump out
of a plane with a parachute
and land close to the fire.

Smoke jumpers training to fight fires.

1

2

3

4

Wire is used to help explode the dynamite.

8

Sometimes buildings have to be
taken down because they are
too old or in the way.
This can be a dangerous job.
The people who do this job
sometimes use dynamite
to blow the building up.
They have to get away quickly
before the building falls down.

Some people are rescue workers.
They have to rescue people
from very dangerous places,
such as from a cliff, in the ocean,
or in caves. Rescue workers have
to be very careful that they don't
get into danger themselves.

cave rescue

cliff rescue

sea rescue

Some people have jobs doing stunts. They do stunts for the actors in a movie. Some stunts are: falling out of a building, jumping through a fire, or jumping out of a plane. These stunts can be very dangerous, so stunt people have to protect themselves and learn how to do the stunts well.

If the stunt is a falling stunt, stunt people use airbags to protect them when they land. If the stunt is jumping through a fire, they will need to wear a suit that will not burn. If the stunt involves jumping out of a plane, the stunt person will have a parachute. Sometimes the parachute is on their back, but sometimes they hold on to it in front of them. This can be very dangerous.

Working with a tiger.

Working with a gorilla.

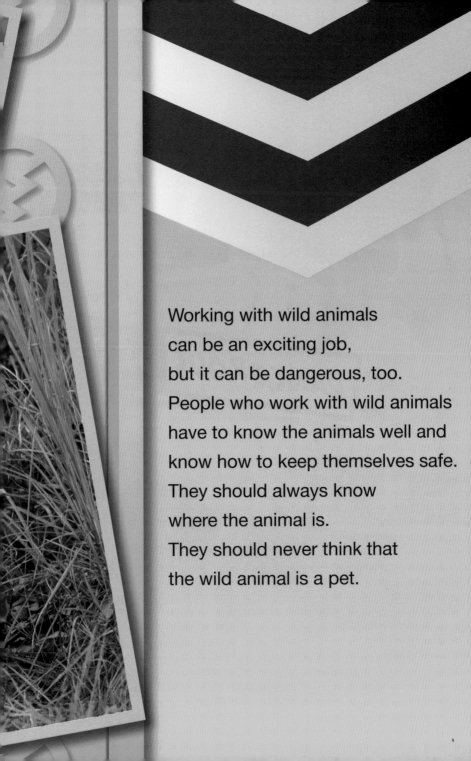

Working with wild animals
can be an exciting job,
but it can be dangerous, too.
People who work with wild animals
have to know the animals well and
know how to keep themselves safe.
They should always know
where the animal is.
They should never think that
the wild animal is a pet.

DANGEROUS JOBS

18

INDEX

Guide Notes

Title: Dangerous Jobs
Stage: Launching Fluency – Orange

Genre: Nonfiction
Approach: Guided Reading
Processes: Thinking Critically, Exploring Language, Processing Information
Written and Visual Focus: Labels, Captions, Photographic Sequences, Index
Word count: 373

THINKING CRITICALLY
(sample questions)
- What jobs do you know that could be dangerous?
- What might you expect to see in this book?
- Look at the index. Encourage the students to think about the information and make predictions about the text content.
- Look at pages 4 and 5. What do you think could make the fire explode?
- Look at pages 6 and 7. Why do you think the fire might be hard to get to?
- Look at the pictures on pages 8 and 9. What other dangers do you think there could be when the building is falling down?
- Look at pages 10 and 11. What dangers do you think the rescue workers could get into themselves?
- Look at pages 14 and 15. Why do you think the stunt person might have to hold on to a parachute in front of them?
- What in the book has helped you understand the information?
- What questions do you have after reading the text?

EXPLORING LANGUAGE

Terminology
Photograph credits, index

Vocabulary
Clarify: dynamite, explode, parachute, stunt, actors
Singular/Plural: job/jobs, person/people, week/weeks, place/places
Homonyms: there/their, through/threw, where/wear